INVASION OF THE SPACE PHANTOMS

INVASION OF THE SPACE PHANTOMS

marvelkids.com

© 2016 MARVEL. All rights reserved. Published by Marvel Press, an imprint of Disney Book Group. No part of this book may be reproduced or transmitted in any form or by any means, electronic or mechanical, including photocopying, recording, or by any information storage or retrieval system, without written permission from the publisher. For information address Marvel Press, 125 West End Avenue, New York, New York 10023.
Printed in the United States of America   First Paperback Edition, March 2016 10 9 8 7 6 5 4 3 2 1 Library of Congress Control Number: 2015917627
FAC-029261-16043   ISBN 978-1-4847-3269-4

Additional illustrations by Ron Lim and Richard Isanove

Cover design by Kurt Hartman
Designed by Jennifer Redding and Betty Avila

SUSTAINABLE FORESTRY INITIATIVE
Certified Sourcing
www.sfiprogram.org
SFI-01415

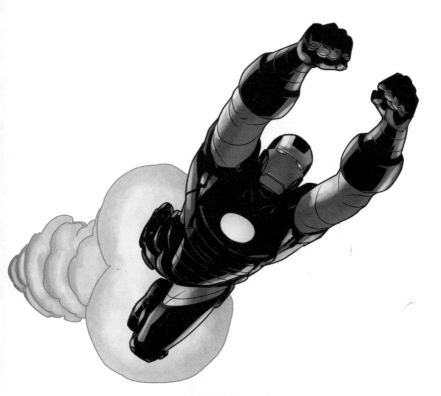

STARRING

IRON MAN

BY *STEVE BEHLING*

ILLUSTRATED BY

KHOI PHAM AND *CHRIS SOTOMAYOR*

Los Angeles
New York

FEATURING YOUR FAVORITES!

IRON MAN

ALIAS

TONY STARK

CAPTAIN AMERICA

FALCON

HULK

M.O.D.O.K.

NICK FURY

BLACK WIDOW

A.I.M. AGENTS

ROBOT SHARKS

PHANTOMS

OUTPOST 13

S.H.I.E.L.D. AGENTS

ALIEN DOGS

**LIVING SNOWMEN
(NOT REALLY)**

**COSMIC BRIDGE
GENERATOR**

THE STORY OF IRON MAN

*I*nventor. Pioneer. Genius. **Tony Stark** is all of the above, and he'd be the first to say so! In fact, he's much more. But let's not get ahead of ourselves.

After the unfortunate death of his father, Howard Stark, Tony became responsible for his father's megasuccessful company,

STARK INDUSTRIES, at only twenty-one years old! Stark Industries developed and built state-of-the-art weapons and sold them around the world. Tony didn't care what happened to the weapons after they were sold; he just wanted to be rich!

Then one fateful day, during a top-secret weapons test, Stark was ambushed by a gang of heavily armed criminals and taken prisoner. He was critically wounded and told he had only a short time to live. With Stark weakened, the criminals forced him to build a weapon for them—a weapon of mass destruction. But Stark had other plans! He forged an incredible suit of armor and a miniature arc reactor to power it and keep his heart beating.

With his new arsenal, Stark defeated the criminals and escaped. He vowed from that day forward that he would use his scientific knowledge to help people all over the world. He upgraded the suit of armor and became the invincible **IRON MAN**!

Iron Man joined Black Widow, Captain America, Hawkeye, the Hulk, and Thor to form the **AVENGERS** — a team of Earth's Mightiest Heroes dedicated to saving the world.

CHAPTER 1

"IS MY BOW TIE STRAIGHT? TELL ME MY BOW TIE IS STRAIGHT,"

Tony said with a groan. *Standing around shaking hands and saying, "Great to see you!" to people I don't even know is hardly my idea of a good time,* he thought. *I'd rather armor up and throw down with the* **Crimson Dynamo**!

Happy Hogan, Tony's bodyguard, let out a loud sigh. "You aren't wearing a bow tie, Boss. Remember? You said you didn't want to look like me." Happy fidgeted in his tuxedo, nervously fixing his own crooked bow tie.

1

"Right, right. So remind me why I agreed to come to this thing?" said Tony. Just then, a voice thundered through the ballroom's public address system.

"Welcome, everyone, and thank you for attending the inaugural benefit for the **Holistic Plan for Tomorrow**!" The crowd of well-dressed partygoers burst into applause as a large hologram of an older man appeared in the center of the room.

"While I am sorry that I am unable to attend in person, I wanted to thank you all for coming. As you know, the Holistic Plan for Tomorrow—**H.P.T.**—is dedicated to opening new doors for the future. With your generous donations, we will create a world the likes of which no one has ever seen!"

The hologram's voice and face belonged to the mysterious **Elton Traggeore**, a reclusive billionaire who was the president of H.P.T.

"HEY, HE'S A RICH GUY, JUST LIKE YOU," said Happy, laughing. "Do you know him?"

"It's not like there's some rich-guy club, Happy," said Tony, rolling his eyes. Happy raised an eyebrow. "Besides, no one's ever met Elton Traggeore."

Before Happy could reply, he and Tony heard a familiar voice. **"Mr. Stark?"**

Turning around, Tony found himself face to face with **Agent Phil Coulson**, a member of the top-secret organization known as **S.H.I.E.L.D.** Coulson smiled at Tony and Happy, gesturing toward the ballroom's exit doors.

"I know that smile," said Tony with a sigh. "That's your 'I'm smiling but I'm not really smiling' smile."

"Would you mind coming with me?" asked Coulson. He pointed once again to the exit.

Tony nodded for Happy to stay as he and Coulson walked out of the ballroom and into the long, crowded entrance hall. Tony spoke quietly. "So what does **S.H.I.E.L.D.** want with Mr. Doesn't-Play-Well-with-Others?" asked Tony. "You guys lose the **Hulk**?"

Coulson looked at Tony. There was no longer a smile on his face, forced or otherwise.

"No," replied Coulson. **"Black Widow and Falcon."**

"Wait, what? *Really?*" said Tony loudly. People in the hallway turned his way suddenly.

Coulson looked down at the ground and whispered, **"We have a . . . problem at OUTPOST 13."**

MISSING

To the public, it was known as **U.S. SCIENCE FOUNDATION OUTPOST 13.** The scientists there, tucked away in the wastelands of Antarctica, claimed to be studying astronomy and surveying the vast shelves of ice. In reality, **OUTPOST 13** was home to an ultra-secret **S.H.I.E.L.D.** research lab.

And that research lab was currently testing a *marvelous* new device . . . invented by Tony Stark.

"Define 'problem,'" said Tony, his curiosity piqued.

"We hadn't received a transmission from Outpost 13 in over a week—but then one came. They kept repeating the words MONSTER and HELP. **Director Fury** sent **Black Widow** and **Falcon** to investigate, but we haven't heard from either of them in forty-eight hours."

Tony stared at Coulson. Falcon and Black Widow were his friends. They were also forces to be reckoned with. Now they were missing. . . .

"I'll go," said Tony. "I can get there faster than anyone."

"Not just you. **You** *and* **Captain America**. You'll rendezvous with Steve Rogers at approximately—"

THUD!

Before Coulson could finish, Tony headed toward the parking lot, where a **STARK INDUSTRIES** vehicle waited. As Coulson picked up his pace in pursuit, Tony opened the trunk of the shiny red car.

"I hear you, Coulson," said Tony, without looking back. **"You have really loud shoes."**

THUD!
THUD!
THUD!
THUD!
THUD!

"Mr. Stark, it's vital that you combine your efforts with **Captain America**," said Coulson as he approached. "This is more than one Avenger can handle . . . even *you*. We sent both Black Widow and Falcon—two of **S.H.I.E.L.D.**'s best—and now they're **MIA**. You'll *need* Rogers on this." Coulson shifted his feet uncomfortably. "Maybe even the **Hulk**."

Without warning, various pieces of metal flew from the trunk toward Tony, attaching themselves to his hands and feet. Within seconds, Tony was encased in a nearly impervious **suit of armor**.

"The research being conducted at **OUTPOST 13** . . . if it should fall into the wrong hands . . ." said Coulson. He glared at Stark, as if he knew exactly what the genius inventor would say.

"I know all about the research, Coulson. They're using my technology. And if Widow, Falcon, or anyone else is hurt because of me, it's my job to make things right."

Where there once stood a billionaire inventor now stood the invincible

IRON MAN!

As the armor powered up, Tony's mind raced. Years before, he had become Iron Man when he realized STARK INDUSTRIES' technology could be used to hurt others. He had since dedicated his life to helping humanity. And now he was faced with a situation where all his efforts could be undone.

"Mr. Stark, wait!" yelled Coulson, but his plea was ignored.

"The *right* hands will make sure the *wrong* hands don't get away with anything. Tell your boss not to worry. It's nothing Iron Man can't handle!" With that, he activated his boot jets and blasted into the night sky.

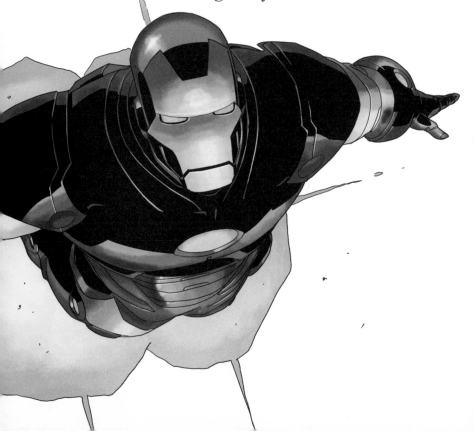

*I*t took Tony a little under six hours' flight time to reach snowy Antarctica. He surveyed the desolate surroundings via his helmet's heads-up display and asked *J.A.R.V.I.S.* to give him the lowdown on the area.

"Temperature: zero degrees Fahrenheit. Atmospheric conditions: currently snowing. Expected snowfall: six inches. Barometer holding st—"

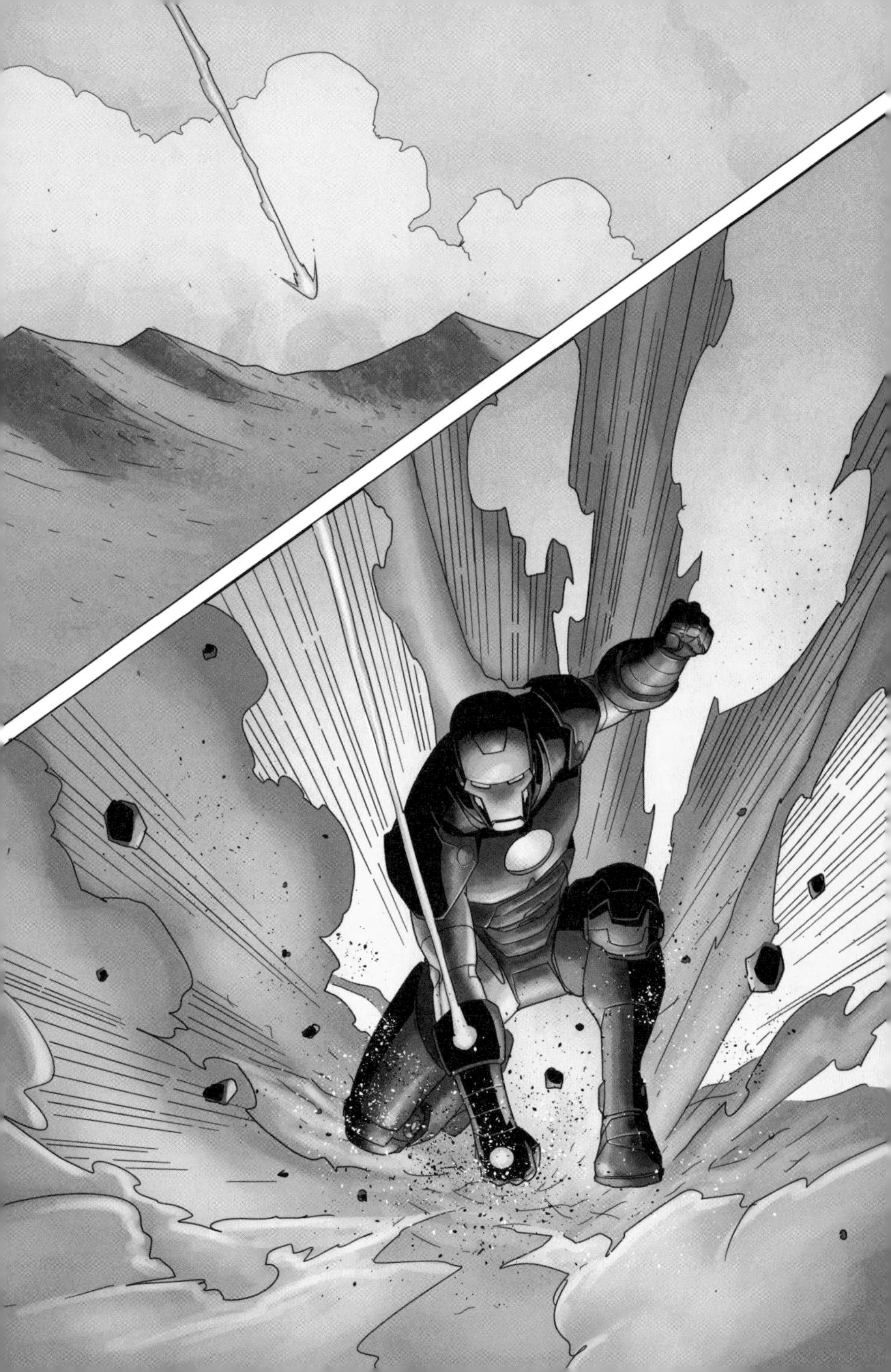

"J.A.R.V.I.S.," said Tony. "Scratch the weatherman bit. How about we start with signs of life?"

A brief humming followed, and *J.A.R.V.I.S.* spoke once more. "Approximately three point two miles southwest.

"_MULTIPLE HEARTBEATS DETECTED—"

*Black Widow, Falcon, the scientists . . .
and what else?*

"*—LIFE-FORMS UNKNOWN.* I'm receiving significant signal interference," finished J.A.R.V.I.S.

"Don't tell me," Tony continued.

"IT'S THE NIGHT OF THE LIVING SNOWMEN, RIGHT?"

"Impossible. It is currently four p.m. local time. And snowmen are not living entities," J.A.R.V.I.S. answered.

Ignoring his armor's operating system, Tony activated his boot jets and unleashed a chemical thrust that propelled him into the air.

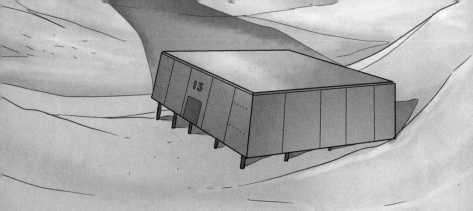

He used his hand repulsors to stabilize and took off in the direction *J.A.R.V.I.S.* had indicated. The heavy snowfall made flying by sight nearly impossible, but his armor's navigation systems quickly took over. Tony zeroed in on a small clearing, where the burnt remains of a rectangular building, with portholes placed every few feet, stood on scorched stilts.

OUTPOST 13.

Tony's armored boots crunched through the snow as he approached the main entrance to the outpost. A chill crept up Tony's spine, and it wasn't from the cold.

No smoke, thought Tony. *This fire happened at least a day ago.* Immediately, his thoughts went to Black Widow and Falcon. *Without the proper gear, surviving the harsh Antarctic environment even an hour is a challenge, let alone two days.* . . .

As Tony approached **OUTPOST 13**, his audio sensors picked up a sound . . . distant and muffled tapping, gaining speed and getting louder, something—some*things*—slamming into the metal interior walls with tremendous force. Suddenly, the door flung off its hinges and three large sled dogs burst from the entrance to **OUTPOST 13**. The canines barked aggressively and bared their fangs.

Their eyes glowed a sinister deep red.

"Whoa, nice doggies!" said Tony, holding his palms out toward the canines. "Uh, roll over! Fetch?" *Where's a stick when you need one?* he thought, moving forward. Before he could take another step, one of the dogs jumped and slammed into his armor, knocking him down. Tony scrambled to his feet as another dog smashed his helmet with its giant front paws. Then the remaining dog started VIBRATING and SHAKING, and one of its large forepaws MORPHED into a long TENTACLE! The appendage wrapped around Tony's right arm and squeezed the armor so tightly that it started to bow and bend under the pressure.

"I don't have dogs, but they don't usually have tentacles, right, *J.A.R.V.I.S.*?" asked Tony.

"AFFIRMATIVE, SIR."

At the *SPEED OF LIGHT*, Tony sent a volley of repulsor blasts from his wrist gauntlets in all directions, causing two of the dogs to scatter behind the outpost, howling. Meanwhile, the third dog continued to squeeze Tony's right arm with its snakelike appendage.

"You can . . . let go . . . anytime you want!" said Tony as he held his left gauntlet right above the dog's limb and emitted a controlled repulsor burst from his palm. The dog let out a shrill squeal and uncoiled its tentacle from Tony's arm.

I'm beginning to see why Coulson was so worried, Tony thought. *If this is just the welcoming committee . . .*

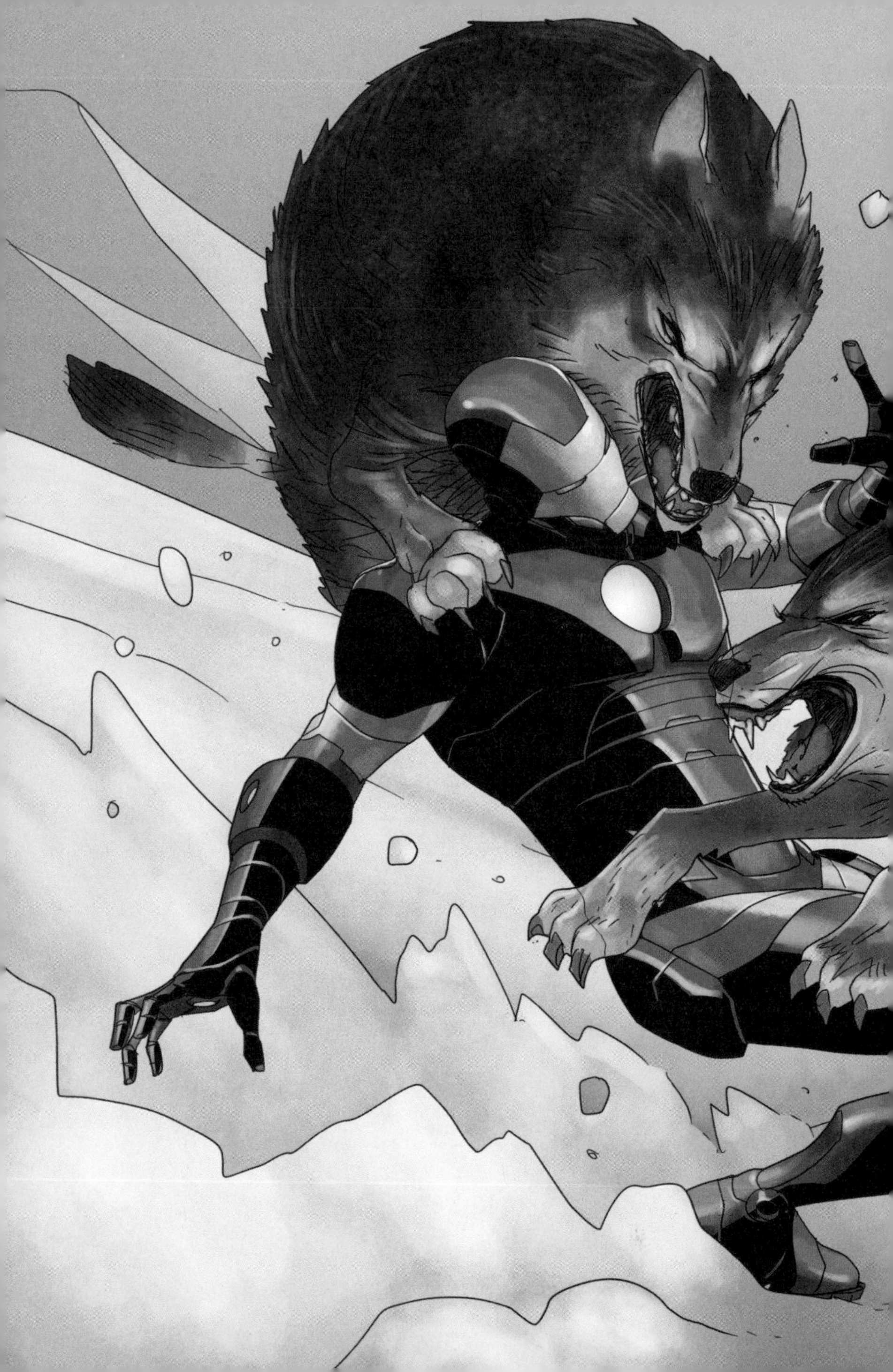

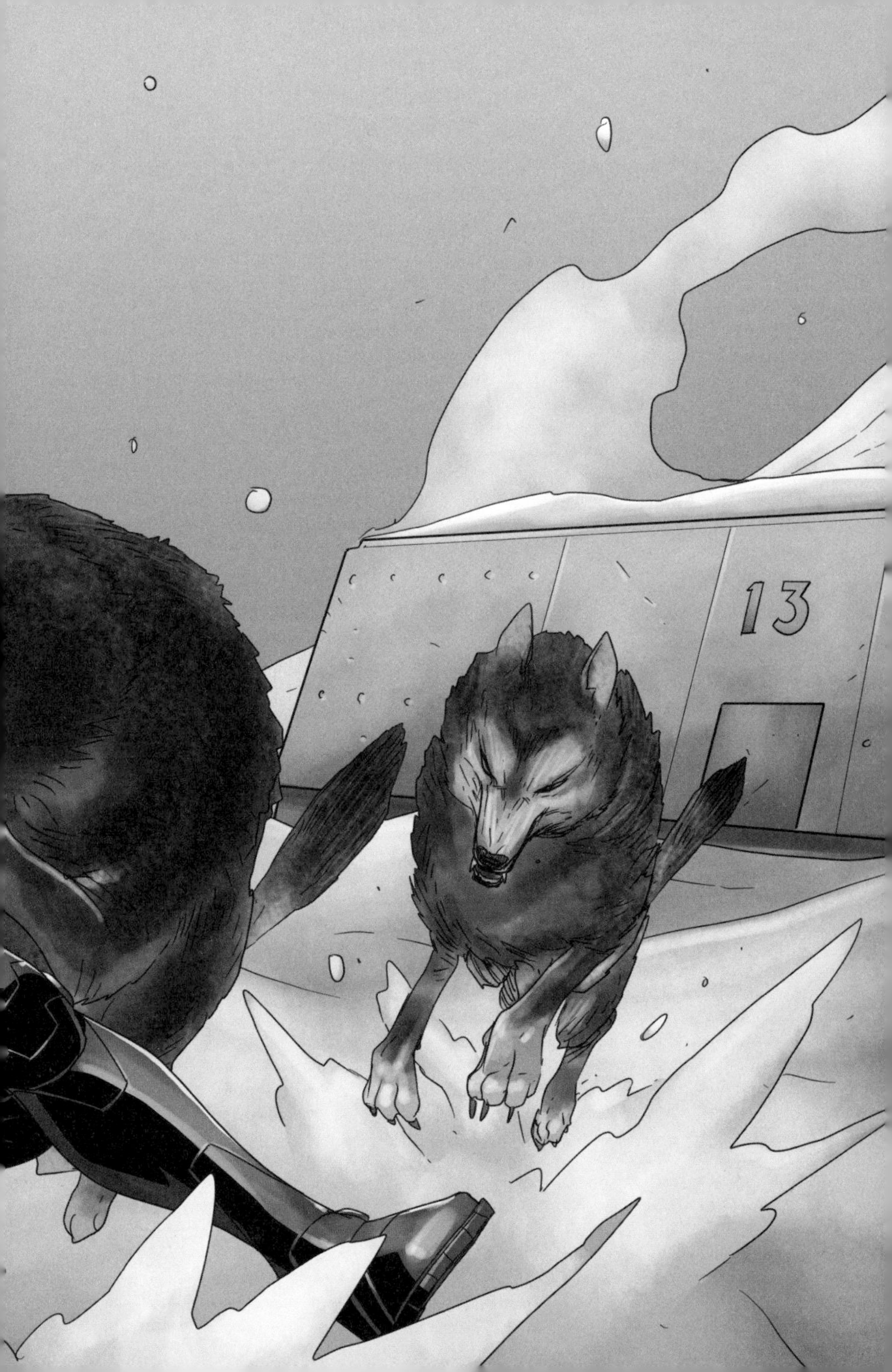
13

The canines continued to change shape, growing in mass until they were nearly three times their original size, with eight tentacles each. They were greenish yellow in color, with glowing red eyes, and their mouths had **barbed tonguelike projections**.

As Tony struggled with his foes, he caught a fleeting look at a face gazing out from one of the outpost portholes. Then another. He looked again and they were gone.

Tony was only minutes into the mission, and the situation was deteriorating rapidly. Dogs that evolved into weird octopus creatures? He worried that these were the threats **Black Widow** and **Falcon** had faced. And could those faces he'd seen belong to some of the missing scientists?

The questions were piling up?

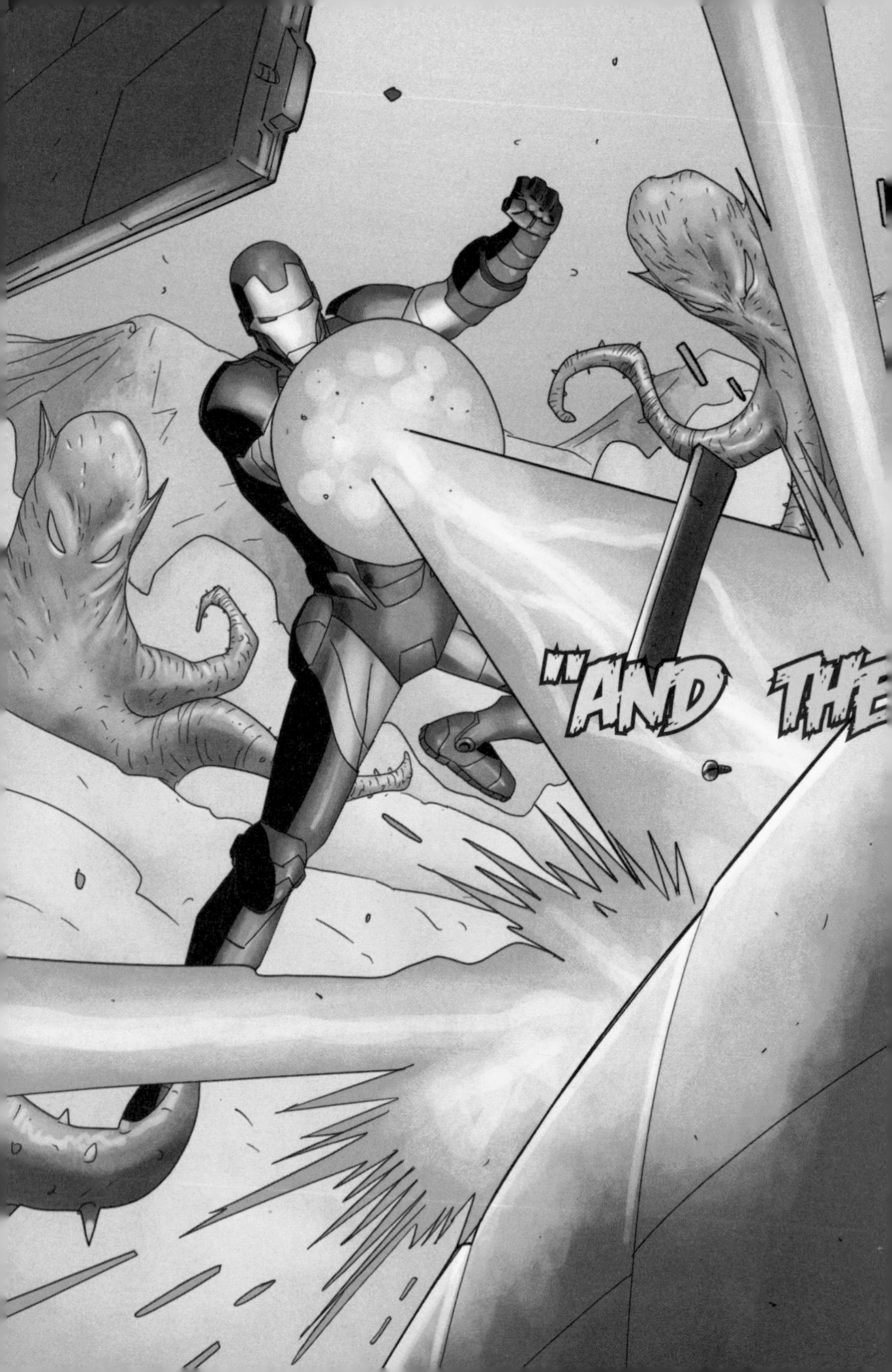
"AND THE

Thinking fast, Tony fired rapid repulsor bursts at the ice mounds the creatures were using as protection, causing them to dive out of the way. Next he fired a blast at a metallic cylinder that extended from OUTPOST 13 into the ice below, ripping open an Iron Man–size hole. Then he activated his boot jets, thrust himself past the beasts, and soared into the cylinder.

FINISHING TOUCH . . ."

said Tony as a brilliant blast of heat issued from his armor's unibeam, sealing the cylinder from the inside.

"This was either a really good idea or a terribly bad one," he said with a laugh. He proceeded through the cylinder and into the darkness below . . . **alone**.

CHAPTER 3

*I*ron Man landed at the bottom of the metallic cylinder and found an opening that led to a hallway of corrugated metal. Dim yellow lights dotted either side of the hallway.

"*J.A.R.V.I.S.*, those things back there. Any idea what they were?" said Tony as he entered the below-freezing hallway.

"*SCANNING DATABASE. RESULT: NEGATIVE. IT MUST BE SOME-THING WE HAVEN'T ENCOUNTERED YET,*" replied *J.A.R.V.I.S.*

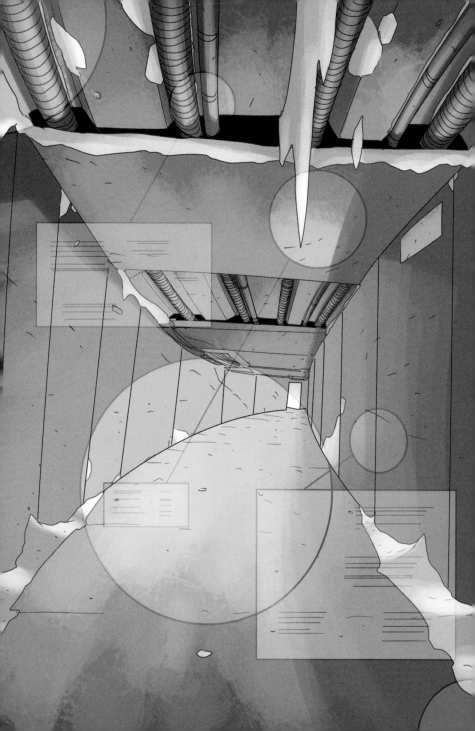

"It must be," said Tony, sighing heavily as he continued down the hallway. He reached a door with a sign above it that read **VAN WALL RESEARCH CENTER**. Curious, he entered, using his helmet's visual scanners to assess the large room. Heavy machinery lined the walls, and a bank of computers that rivaled anything on the **S.H.I.E.L.D.** Helicarrier stood in the middle. The scanners revealed energy **WAVELENGTHS** that were familiar to him.

As Tony walked toward the computers, **J.A.R.V.I.S.** blared in his ears: **"LIFE-FORM DETECTED."**

Whirling around, Tony zeroed in on a metal storage unit in a far corner. He was getting a little tired of this game of **hide-and-seek**.

"**Whoever's in that cabinet can come on out,**" called Tony. "It'll save us both some time."

The cabinet door whipped open, and out staggered a frumpy middle-aged man.

"**IRON MAN!**" he said, running toward the armored Avenger.

Iron Man steadied the man, bracing his shoulders with both hands. Tony decided to slide his metal visor back, revealing his face. "Take it easy, **Dr. . . . Blair**," said Tony as he read the badge on the man's lab coat. "Where are the missing scientists? Where—"

Blair grabbed Iron Man's wrist, tugging him in the opposite direction. **"I'm the only one! We need to leave, now!"**

"You're safe, Dr. Blair," said Tony, trying his best to sound reassuring. "I need some answers. Where is everyone? What were you working on?"

The doctor wrung his hands nervously, sweating profusely. "Our—our research . . ." he stammered. **"The Cosmic Bridge Generator—"**

"A portal," interrupted Tony, **"to another, unseen dimension.** A way of harnessing extraterrestrial power sources for the benefit of everyone on Earth."

Blair nodded. "The first test knocked out our communications. We spent days trying to get them up and running. That's when Black Widow and Falcon arrived. **Without warning, they attacked us!**"

J.A.R.V.I.S. suddenly spoke in Tony's ear. "I am detecting a rise in Dr. Blair's blood pressure and heart rate."

He's lying, thought Tony. *Why would Black Widow and Falcon respond to the distress call only to turn around and attack a bunch of scientists?* ***Something's not right. . . .***

Suddenly, a blast of energy hit Tony squarely in the chest plate, knocking him off balance. A glance at the doorway revealed the source of the attack—**Black Widow**. It must have been Tony's imagination, but she seemed so angry her eyes glowed red! Swooping in above her came **Falcon**.

"Black Widow! Falcon!"

Tony faced his teammates. "Coulson's been looking everywhere for you two. What is going on here?

"Ease up, it's me!"

Without a word, Widow fired more bursts from the Widow's Bite gauntlets she wore on her wrists. Intense electric bolts attacked Tony's armor. Various internal alarms sounded, and Tony glanced at his helmet's heads-up display. "'Power cell A compromised'?

That can't be good," said Tony as he crouched in a defensive posture.

"I just had this suit polished!" Tony shouted at Black Widow. His faceplate slid into place, forming the visage of Iron Man. Black Widow said nothing, keeping her glare and her gauntlets trained on him. Falcon's shadow circled them.

"I thought we were fighting on the same team, or am I wrong about that?" Iron Man said, trying to reason with them. But he was met with only an eerie silence and red eyes. Those piercing red eyes. *It's like they're not themselves! Black Widow and Falcon would never*

WHERE'S CAP WHEN YOU NEED HIM?

attack a friend like this. What happened? Or . . .
what happened to *them?*

"Get behind me, Doc!" shouted Iron Man.

The room seemed to spin as **Black Widow** and **Falcon** circled Iron Man and Dr. Blair. Tony took a big gulp. *"It's nothing Iron Man can't handle."* Me and my big mouth.

CHAPTER 4

*I*n the confines of the **VAN WALL RESEARCH CENTER**, Tony was at a disadvantage. Between Black Widow's blasts and Falcon's swooping, circling, and smashing, Tony was getting crushed. Just as he'd right himself, he'd be hit with another attack.

The ceiling was high but not high enough for powered flight. Falcon could glide, so he had the tactical advantage. Black Widow used her expert acrobatics and leapt across the enormous machines that lined the walls.

Tony just couldn't match the speed and agility of Black Widow or Falcon. On top of that, the only way he could defend himself was to hurt his friends. But what kind of friends attacked their own?

"Multiple life-forms detected," declared *J.A.R.V.I.S.*, distracting Tony for a moment . . . which was all Falcon needed to swoop down and grab Iron Man. Falcon flung Tony into a solid granite wall.

Then came the sound of something hurtling through the air, followed by metal hitting metal.

Tony looked up to see a familiar **RED, WHITE, AND BLUE** uniform standing before him. **Captain America!** Black Widow and Falcon turned their combined gaze on Cap.

Cap adjusted the shield on his left arm, deflecting one of Widow's blasts. "I was supposed to catch a ride with you," Cap said.

"I was just on my way to pick you up," Tony said with a sigh of relief.

"I'm glad to see you found Black Widow and Falcon. **They just don't look too glad to see you. . . .** Did you find the scientists?"

"Negative," Tony answered. "Not sure if you noticed, but I've been a little busy fighting our 'friends.'"

"Point taken . . ." replied Cap.

Falcon and Black Widow charged toward them. Cap used his mighty shield to block the two and send them flying.

"Those two seem very interested in this," said Cap, motioning to a circular framework at the center of the room. Inside the framework was a large gateway—big enough to fit the Hulk—surrounded by a series of metal beams that protruded at odd angles. Within the gateway was a swirl of light against dark, color against black. It looked like the universe itself was contained there.

"Oh, no! It's the Cosmic Bridge Generator," Tony said. "I invented it."

"They haven't taken their eyes off it,"

said Cap.

Eyes . . . eyes . . . thought Tony. **Eyes! That's it!**

"Cap! You notice something off about Widow and Falcon?" he asked.

The sentinel of liberty stood his ground, deflecting Widow's attack while taking note of everything around him. It was a skill honed in combat, from his days battling **RED SKULL** and **HYDRA** to his time fighting alongside the mighty Avengers. "Their eyes," Cap answered with authority. "They're red!"

"Good guess!" said Tony. "I owe you shawarma when we're back in New York. Now I've got a hunch. . . ."

Without skipping a beat, Captain America extended his right arm with incredible force, throwing his shield directly at

HELP!

HELP!

HELP!

THUMP!

THUMP!

Falcon's hard-light wings. "Play your hunch!" he called. "I'll draw their fire!"

That's when Tony heard it—a distant thumping, mixed in with what sounded like moans or cries for help. *The scientists? Maybe I did see their faces before. They must be nearby!*

While Captain America fought, Iron Man moved to the metal gateway in the middle of the room. Tony flipped up the cuff on his right gauntlet to access a touch pad. Moving his index finger along the pad, he hacked into the generator's controls. Tony was now in command of the machine.

It glowed purple, then green, and finally red, crackling with orbs of black energy.

"Hey! Bad teammates! Over here!" shouted Iron Man, waving at Black Widow and Falcon.

The generator pulsed, red light illuminating everything in the room. Bathed in the light, Black Widow and Falcon cringed, their shapes shifting then returning to normal. The red light glowed stronger and stronger, and its effect on Black Widow and Falcon grew stronger, too!

Without warning, Iron Man zapped Black Widow and Falcon with his repulsors, knocking them in front of the Cosmic Bridge Generator. In a flash, they both vanished from view.

"Did we just lose Black Widow and Falcon . . . again?" Cap said, shaking his head. "Fury won't like this. What's going on, Tony?"

Iron Man looked at Cap, then at the generator. He had gambled with the lives of people he had known for years. If he was right, then everything would be fine. But what if . . .

What if I was wrong? he thought. *What if I made a mistake?* **What if I have lost Black Widow and Falcon . . . forever?**

CHAPTER

5

*T*he Cosmic Bridge Generator quivered and hummed, its crimson glow permeating everything around it. Captain America ducked behind his shield, eyes closed tightly. Even then he could see the brilliant red light coming from the generator. Tony lowered polarized lenses over the eye ports on his helmet. He couldn't escape the otherworldly red, either.

"There!" said Iron Man as he tapped a sequence into the keypad on his right gauntlet.

He sounded more confident than he felt. Just as quickly as it had started, the generator powered down. **The quivering and humming stopped, and the red glow faded.** Raising the polarized lenses inside his helmet, Tony looked toward the generator. Standing before it were two figures. *What if I just made everything worse?*

"Anyone get the license plate of that truck?"

asked Falcon, rubbing his head. Beside him stood Black Widow. Both heroes looked stunned, unsure of their surroundings.

"You guys all right?" asked Iron Man as he turned to face Widow. He was relieved to see that her eyes were back to normal. Tony Stark raised his visor and grinned. *That was close. . . .*

"I'm fine, Tony," answered Widow. "I just can't remember anything that happened since we arrived at **OUTPOST 13** and were attacked."

Falcon nodded. "Last thing I remember is entering **OUTPOST 13**. We were ambushed by a beast with lots of long slimy arms. Then there was a flash of red, and the next minute—**WHAM**—here we are!"

"Someone activated the generator and it knocked you guys out and sucked you inside . . . into another dimension," Tony explained. "The Falcon and Black Widow who attacked me and Cap? **Doppelgängers. Duplicates. Imitations.**"

The heroes swiveled their heads in unison as they heard the generator hum back to life. Standing in the breached wall was Dr. Blair, looking panicked. He was moving his finger over a device that resembled a wristwatch.

"Can you shut that down, Doc?" groaned Tony.

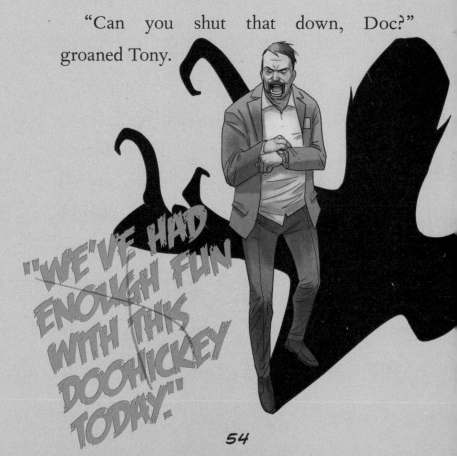

"WE'VE HAD ENOUGH FUN WITH THIS DOOHICKEY TODAY."

"You have to stop them, Iron Man!" blurted Dr. Blair, sounding hysterical. "Those two destroyed Outpost 13! They captured all the S.H.I.E.L.D. scientists!"

"Who's this quack?" asked Falcon, jerking a thumb at the doctor.

Black Widow studied Dr. Blair carefully. "I've never seen you before," she said warily.

Dr. Blair looked at Tony, shaking his head. **"Don't trust them, Iron Man! They were so quick to turn on us before, so ready to attack! What if they do it again?"** He slowly started walking toward Tony.

"Take a deep breath, Doc," said Tony.

The doctor eyed Black Widow and Falcon with suspicion. **"You have to destroy them, Iron Man**—while we still can!"

"Doc, you really need to relax! The Black Widow and Falcon we were fighting before were imitations. These are the real deal."

"Yes, they are," grunted Dr. Blair.

Blair's arm suddenly turned into a tentacle and grabbed Iron Man, smacking him to the ground! The appendage dripped with thick slime and left a sticky green residue on

everything it touched. Wrapping around Iron
Man's helmet, the tentacle began to squeeze
tighter and tighter.

As Tony struggled to free himself, the
Avengers raced to his side. More tentacles
exploded from Blair's body and snaked out in
all directions, stopping the heroes dead in their
tracks. Unleashing two repulsor blasts that hit
Blair in the stomach, Iron Man knocked the
doctor back into the massive machinery. Blair
eased his grip just enough for Tony to escape.

Dr. Blair's shape began to SWELL and DEFORM like a marshmallow in a microwave oven. The mass reformed until it was a large yellow-green blob with eight long appendages. Its eyes glowed red with hate.

"That's something you don't see every day," said Falcon.

The creature unleashed TWO ARMS at **Black Widow**, trying to wrap them around her wrists. But her lightning-fast reflexes kicked in, and she fired off several shots from her Widow's Bite gauntlets. The electric bolts hit the creature and scorched its tentacles.

The beast LASHED out once more, this time at **Captain America**. In one

fluid motion, Cap hurled his shield at the creature's head and then hit the ground in a somersault, ducking below its eight limbs. Cap came out of the roll and firmly planted his fist in its face.

The pulsating mass towered over the Avengers and spoke with venom.

"I AM NOT OF THIS WORLD."

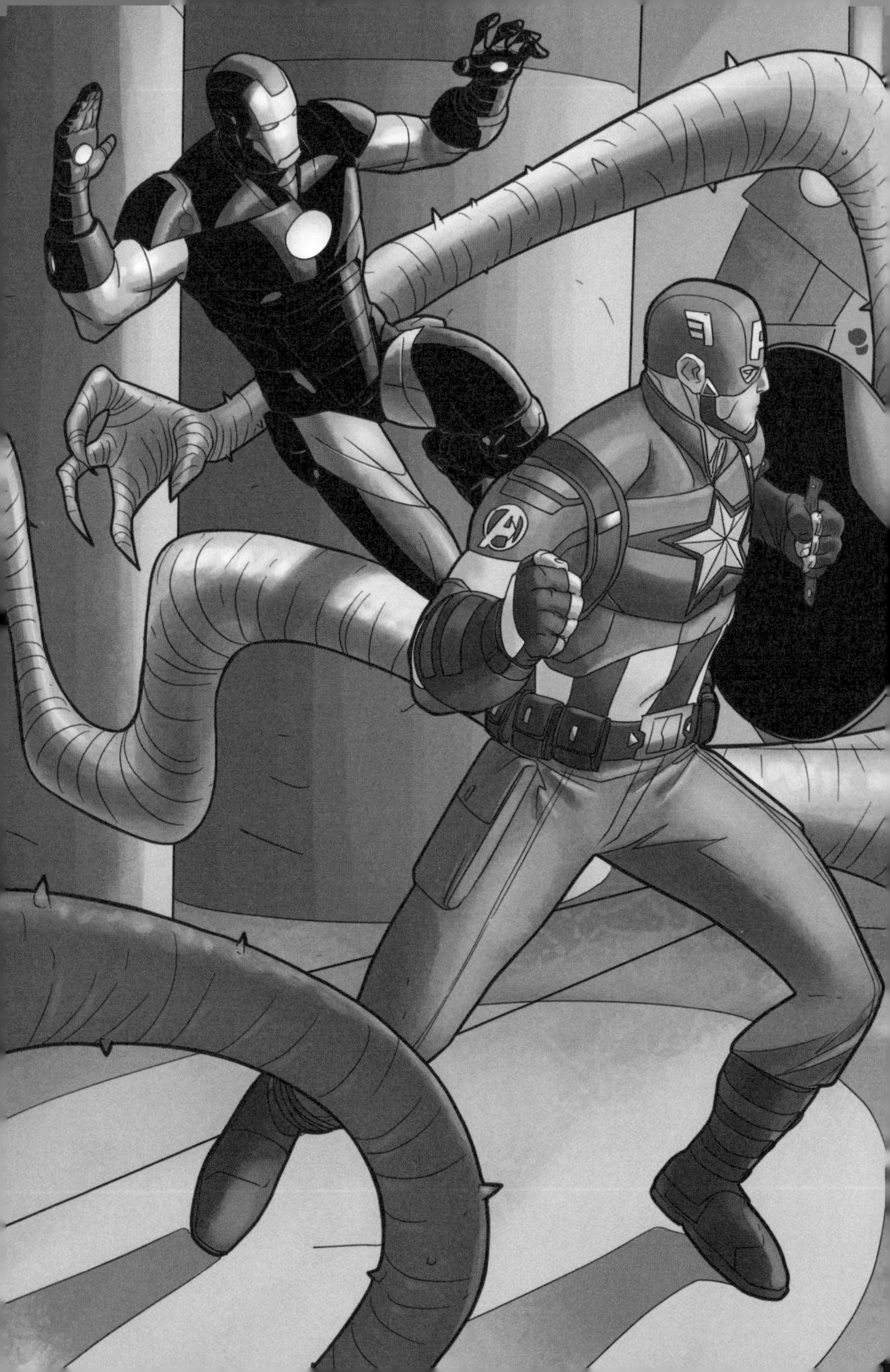

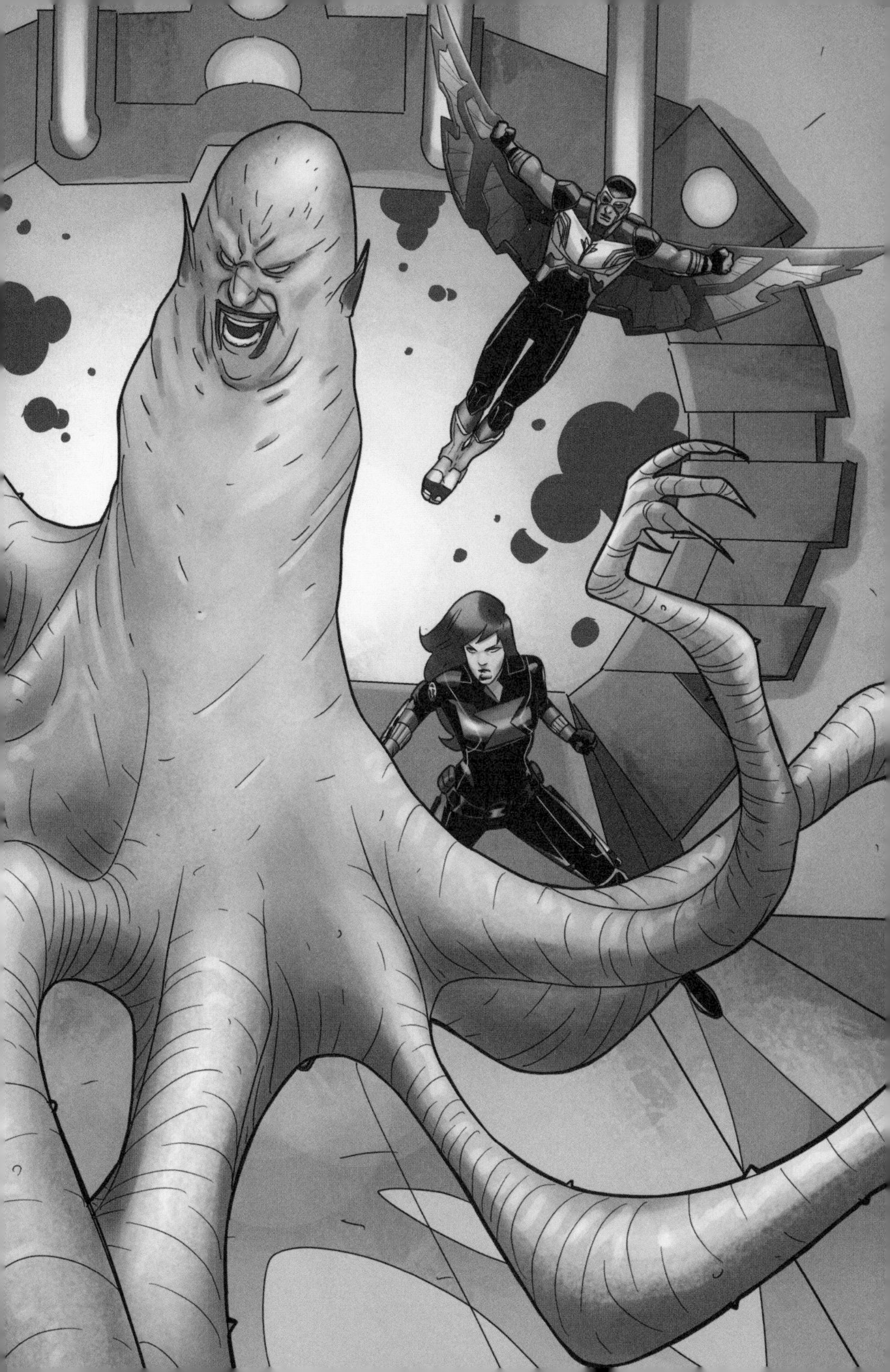

Tony walked closer to the creature as the other Avengers closed in behind him, ready for battle. **The Cosmic Bridge Generator** hummed. "This," began Tony, nodding toward the apparatus, "is pretty important to you, huh?"

The twisted shape spat out its barbed tongue in disgust. "YOU'LL HAVE NO ANSWER FROM ME, HUMAN."

Its raspy voice made Tony's flesh crawl.

"Fair enough," Tony concluded, then whirled around and blasted the generator to pieces with his repulsors. Captain America hurled his shield, smashing the flying debris. As Tony's visor slid into place, Iron Man and

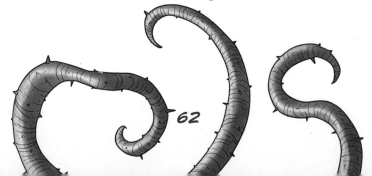

the creature continued their face-off.

The creature smiled. "Do you think that is it?" it hissed. "We are great in number, human! Even as I speak, we near the completion of a new Cosmic Bridge Generator, large enough to bring all of my kind to this pitiful speck of a planet. WE WILL DESTROY ANYTHING IN OUR WAY!"

*T*he room fell silent. The **AVENGERS** stared at the monster before them. No one said anything, but Tony knew what they were thinking: if he hadn't invented the **Cosmic Bridge Generator**, Tony and his teammates wouldn't be staring down the barrel of the end of the world.

I created the generator to do good, Tony thought. *Now it's being turned into something terrible. All right, Mr. Guy-Who-Can-Fix-Anything. How do you fix this?*

Before he could continue his thoughts, Tony heard a banging sound once more and what could have been a muffled cry for help. *The* **S.H.I.E.L.D.** *scientists!* Tony finally pieced together what had happened at **OUTPOST 13**. *These creatures must have captured the scientists and kept them around in case anything went wrong with the generator. They're here somewhere!*

Tony turned to Black Widow and Falcon and with a nod motioned them to the slimy yellow-green beast's side. "Mind telling us what that sound is, gruesome? I'm betting it's the missing **S.H.I.E.L.D.** scientists. Be a good little monster and show us where they are."

"It matters little," sneered the creature as it folded two of its tentacles together. **"YOU CANNOT STOP US."**

"Yeah," said Falcon. "We've heard that one before."

Black Widow and Falcon grabbed the hideous monster and pushed it into the hallway outside, demanding that it lead them toward the captured scientists.

Iron Man stared at the smoldering ruins of the generator. "The more I think about it, there was no way the scientists and that creature could pull this off alone," he mused. "They had to have had help. Someone good at sci crime, maybe."

"'Sci crime'?" said Cap, puzzled.

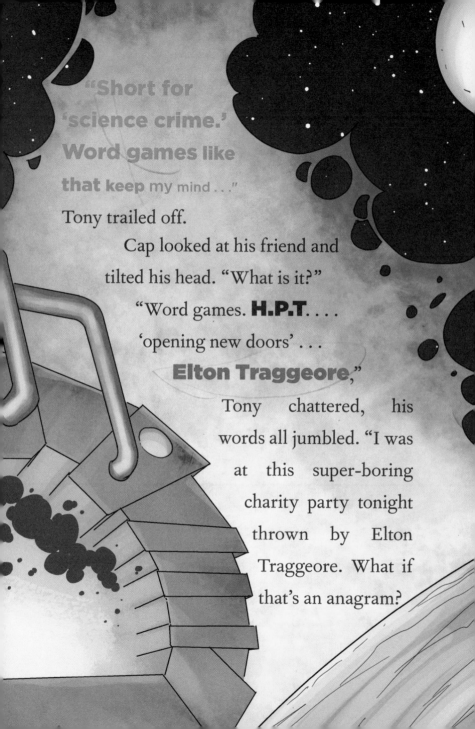

"Short for 'science crime.' Word games like that keep my mind . . ."

Tony trailed off.

Cap looked at his friend and tilted his head. "What is it?"

"Word games. **H.P.T.** . . . 'opening new doors' . . . **Elton Traggeore**," Tony chattered, his words all jumbled. "I was at this super-boring charity party tonight thrown by Elton Traggeore. What if that's an anagram?

"Rearrange the letters in Elton Traggeore and you get another name: **George Tarleton**. George Tarleton, as in . . ."

Cap and Iron Man looked at each other and spoke in unison:

"M.O.D.O.K."

By the time **Iron Man** and **Captain America** caught up with Black Widow and Falcon, the two heroes had found and freed the missing **S.H.I.E.L.D.** scientists. Two of the scientists, Agent MacReady and Agent Childs, were prepping a cryo-containment unit to hold the creature. The unit—a sleek translucent tube with metal caps—would keep its occupant in a state of suspended animation:

alive, **asleep,**

and unable to do any damage.

The monster fixed its eyes on Agents Childs and MacReady. Tony approached from behind and opened his chest unibeam, which unleashed a blast that knocked the monster into the cryo-containment unit. The creature bounced back immediately, and Tony gulped. *No one gets up from a full unibeam hit that fast. Not even Thor.* "PATHETIC EARTHLING. NOTHING YOU DO CAN STOP US. NOTHING!"

"Childs, MacReady, get this thing out of here!" said Tony.

"With pleasure," Childs replied as she activated the cryo-containment unit. With a *whoosh*, the unit sealed itself, flash-freezing the monster inside. Anti-gravity discs beneath the unit turned on and the capsule **HOVERED** just above the floor.

"One alien on ice ready for transport," said MacReady. He and Childs gave the unit a push and slowly maneuvered it out the door.

Tony's mind turned to **M.O.D.O.K.** The villain never worked alone.

A.I.M. and **M.O.D.O.K.** Two of Iron Man's oldest enemies.

A.I.M.

ADVANCED IDEA MECHANICS

was a criminal organization that used science for evil. It was that science that had transformed a lowly A.I.M. agent named George Tarleton into **M.O.D.O.K.** He had then turned the tables on A.I.M., using his superintelligent brain to take over the organization. M.O.D.O.K.'s mind powers could be deadly, and everyone knew it. The A.I.M. agents obeyed his every order. Luckily, sensitive scanners in Iron Man's armor could locate M.O.D.O.K.'s energy signature and track him anywhere.

Tony paused and looked down at his armor-covered hands—the brilliant crimson gloves that could forge reality from dreams. But dreams could become nightmares. An unfamiliar feeling seized him: guilt.

I invented the generator. And now the bad guys are going to use it to mess with the earth. This is all my fault. I have to fix this mess myself.

"All right, people," Cap ordered. **"We need a battle plan and—"**

"Plan whatever you want," said Tony, cutting off Captain America. "I'm taking **M.O.D.O.K.** down. Now."

BATTLE PLAN:

REALLY
GOOD
BATTLE
PLAN
US
THEM

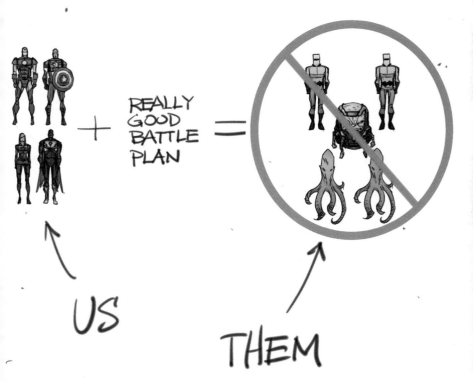

The high-pitched whine of Iron Man's boot
jets kicked in, and Cap jumped back. He yelled
over the sound of chemical thrust, "You can't
defeat M.O.D.O.K. by yourself!"

But Tony wasn't listening. The armored Avenger blasted off, arms outstretched, and used his repulsors to smash through the roof above.

Iron Man was gone!

CHAPTER

7

"*E*TA, J.A.R.V.I.S.?" asked Tony, sweating inside his armor despite the temperature control.

"*ESTIMATED TIME OF ARRIVAL THREE MINUTES, THREE SECONDS*," J.A.R.V.I.S. replied.

Tony checked his visual scanners as he skimmed the surface of the Atlantic Ocean— low enough to evade any **A.I.M.** radar. Almost as if on cue, A.I.M. Island appeared on the horizon.

"Let's go for a swim, _J.A.R.V.I.S._," said Tony. In response, J.A.R.V.I.S. immediately prepped the armor for underwater maneuvers. All openings were sealed; carbon dioxide exhaust ports were activated.

Tony plunged into the ocean.

Why did I snap at Cap back there? he thought.

Tiny caterpillar drives—silent engines—turned in Tony's boots, propelling him toward A.I.M. Island with stunning speed. In the quiet ocean void, Tony gave himself over to his thoughts.

I wasn't angry with him. I was angry with myself. None of this is his fault. If I hadn't built the generator in the first place, those aliens wouldn't be trying to take over the earth. And M.O.D.O.K. *and* A.I.M. *wouldn't be helping them.*

Once again, Tony was overwhelmed with guilt. How could he continue to invent advanced technologies but also guarantee they would be used only for good and not evil— **to help others, not hurt them**?

He checked his oxygen supply— 85 percent. So far, so good. The armor's motion detectors revealed three objects circling in the distance. Sharks, maybe? But J.A.R.V.I.S. hadn't detected any life-forms. 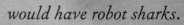ROBOT SHARKS, *I bet. Of course* A.I.M. *would have robot sharks.*

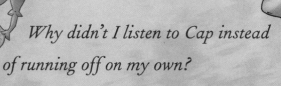

Why didn't I listen to Cap instead of running off on my own?

Tony activated his armor's underwater countermeasures, and several small robotic beacons ejected from his shoulder launcher. Each mimicked the sounds of Tony's armor and drew two of the robot sharks away. The third shark was HUNGRY ... for metal! It attacked Tony from below and almost swallowed him whole! THE METAL TEETH GROUND AGAINST HIS ARMOR, and his suit began to fizzle and cave in on him. Tony quickly grabbed the robotic jaws and activated his elbow thrusters, tearing the metal mouth in two.

Really? Tony thought. *I almost bit the bullet because of a* ROBO—FISH? He rocketed like a torpedo toward his destination.

Beneath the ocean, A.I.M. Island looked like a large geodesic dome constructed of foreign materials—nothing like the islands Tony was used to vacationing at.

This is where Cap would say, **"We need a plan. We need to act as a team,"** thought Tony. *And here I am with neither. Well done, Stark, well done.*

"Okay," Tony said to himself, "time to make a door."

"They kind of give me the creeps," said the A.I.M. agent with a shudder. She stood with another agent at the door of a large control room.

"*Shhhh,*" the second agent replied softly. "Don't let the boss hear you talking like that!"

ZAAAAAAK! The wall ripped open, torn apart by a massive repulsor blast! In rushed a torrent of seawater and, along with it, Iron Man! The agents were knocked unconscious. An alarm wailed for only a second before it was silenced by Iron Man's repulsor.

Let's hope I didn't wake anybody up, he thought.

Within minutes, the wall had resealed, leaving no sign of Iron Man's entrance. **"Self-healing polymer walls,"** said Tony. "We'll have to look into those for Stark Tower. Save a fortune every time the Hulk busts a wall."

Iron Man was inside **A.I.M.**'s hidden base, in a **twisting** corridor. Activating his boot jets, Tony took off, continuing to follow **M.O.D.O.K.**'s energy signature.

—●—

The master control room is enormous, Tony thought. He was up in an air shaft, looking down at the room through a grate. He saw an assembly of **A.I.M.** agents—all armed—surrounding an enormous duplicate **Cosmic Bridge Generator**.

"You are too cautious," said a spine-chilling voice.

"And you are not cautious enough!" came the reply, silencing everyone in the room.

Tony took a second to place the first voice, but he knew the second one.... **M.O.D.O.K.**

Iron Man smirked. He was confident he had the element of surprise. He prepared to blast through the grate, but before he could act, an explosion struck Tony's hiding spot. He fell to the floor of the master control room, hard.

"You're late, Iron Man," M.O.D.O.K. intoned. He almost sounded bored. "I EXPECTED YOU APPROXIMATELY THIRTY-FOUR SECONDS AGO."

Iron Man righted himself and was greeted by the army of A.I.M. agents. Floating beside them in his hover chair was M.O.D.O.K. His head was impossibly huge and his limbs tiny, almost useless. In the center of his vast forehead was a glowing beam, the source of his immense psionic powers.

"I would have been here sooner, but the traffic was terrible," Tony joked. He tried to sound like his usual devil-may-care self, but the odds were against him. Things didn't look good for one lone Iron Man.

M.O.D.O.K. ignored Iron Man and hovered over to the generator's control panels. Iron Man saw the familiar yellow-green blobs, their many arms reaching, grabbing, constructing. This new Cosmic Bridge Generator dwarfed the one Tony had destroyed at **OUTPOST 13**.

"That thing looks big enough to, I don't know, bring a whole planet of slimy, scummy creatures to Earth," said Tony. Channeling as much power as he could to his repulsors, he unleashed a barrage of devastating blasts at the generator. Well, they should have been devastating. Unlike the generator at **OUTPOST 13**, this one was unaffected by his repulsors.

One of the beasts let out a bitter laugh, then slowly shuffled its mass toward Iron Man. Its writhing arms shot out and grabbed

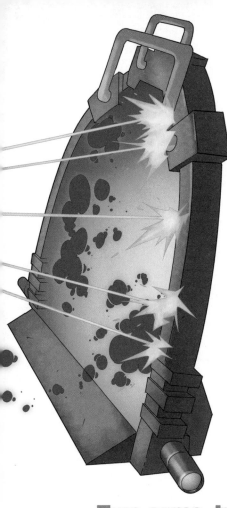

Tony by the neck. Then, without warning, it dropped him and began to change shape. Its features slowly morphed, going from altogether alien to a little more . . . familiar.

Two arms, two legs. Tall. Elongated facial features. Almost human.

Something Tony had seen years before.

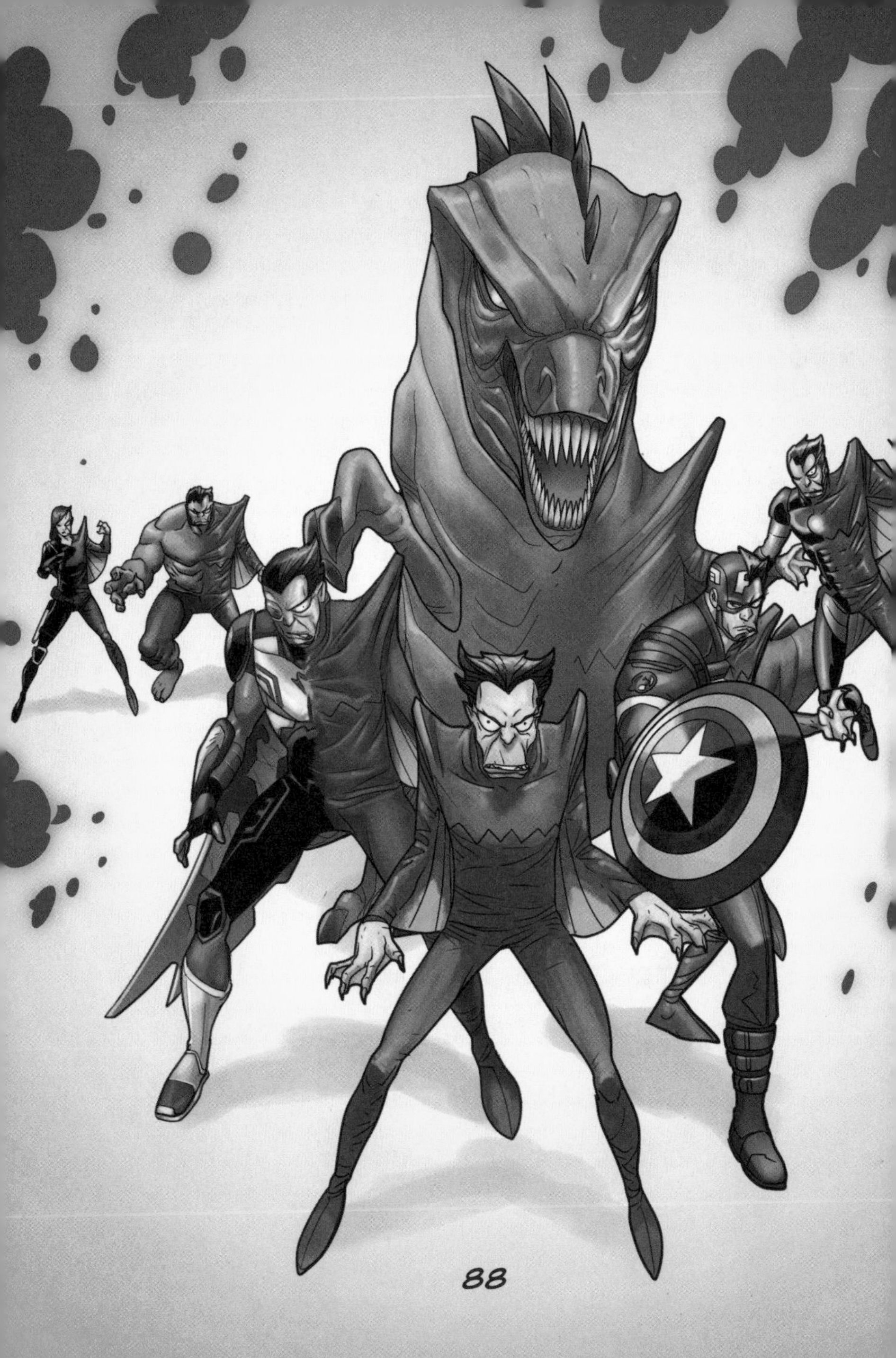

"Phantoms?" said Tony in disbelief. Back when the AVENGERS had first joined together to fight evil, he had encountered a strange being who called himself the Space Phantom. He could change his shape to mimic almost anyone or anything. He imitated the different members of the Avengers, pitting the heroes against one another.

"Yes, that is what your kind call us," snarled the alien, its voice practically dripping with slime. "Our own world has become . . . inhospitable. But your world . . . your Earth . . . will make a glorious new home. Once you and your miserable kind have been . . . displaced."

"**Slow down, sloppy joe. What about all the nice people who already live here?**" Tony asked. The **A.I.M.** agents began to circle Iron Man. Tony's audio sensors detected the sound of their weapons heating up.

"The Phantoms shall first replace all those humans in positions of power," **M.O.D.O.K.** explained. "Your Cosmic Bridge Generator will transport the Phantoms here and send their human counter-parts to their destroyed home world."

That explains why they needed

the generator! Every time a Phantom imitates someone, that person is sent to the Phantom's world. But when a Phantom changes its shape again, the person returns. They would need some other method to send people away permanently . . . *like the generator!*

"And what's in it for you and A.I.M.?" Tony asked M.O.D.O.K.

M.O.D.O.K. threw Tony a look of annoyance. **"IS IT NOT OBVIOUS? I DESIRE COMPLETE CONTROL OF THIS WORLD.** With the Phantoms, that goal is within my grasp."

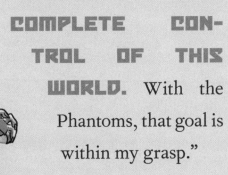

Tony had heard enough. He ordered J.A.R.V.I.S. to switch all energy reserves to his repulsors. But just as he was about to unleash all the force he could muster, he was struck by the **A.I.M.** agents! They fired at once, encasing him in a field of hard light.

Then **J.A.R.V.I.S.** came online with more bad news: "Power now operating at reserve levels."

M.O.D.O.K. and the Phantoms closed in on Tony.

He struggled against the onslaught, but he could still hear Cap's words echoing in his head:

This is too big for any one of us, Tony.

*T*he heads-up display inside Tony Stark's helmet was full of alarms, warnings, and worse. Systems were malfunctioning. Circuits were overloading. Tony knew his armor was crashing.

ALARM!

WARNINGS!

WORSE!

"You delay the inevitable," muttered M.O.D.O.K., who hadn't even bothered to join the fight. The A.I.M. agents' new weapons were doing a good job of destroying Iron Man's armor all on their own. And the Space Phantom smirked at Tony all the while, confident that soon his comrades would begin their takeover of Earth.

"J.A.R.V.I.S.! Reroute all remaining power to the unibeam!" shouted Tony.

"REMAINING POWER REROUTED," said J.A.R.V.I.S.

"Good. Stand by to detonate

unibeam on my mark!'"

Then it happened—so fast that neither **M.O.D.O.K.**, the Phantoms, nor the **A.I.M.** agents could process it:

Tony ejected himself from the Iron Man armor and threw himself across the room, clear of the hard-light bubble and away from his foes.

The armor remained inside the bubble and the unibeam exploded with pent-up energy, shattering its hard-light prison and bathing the room in a shockwave that floored everyone and everything.

—◦—

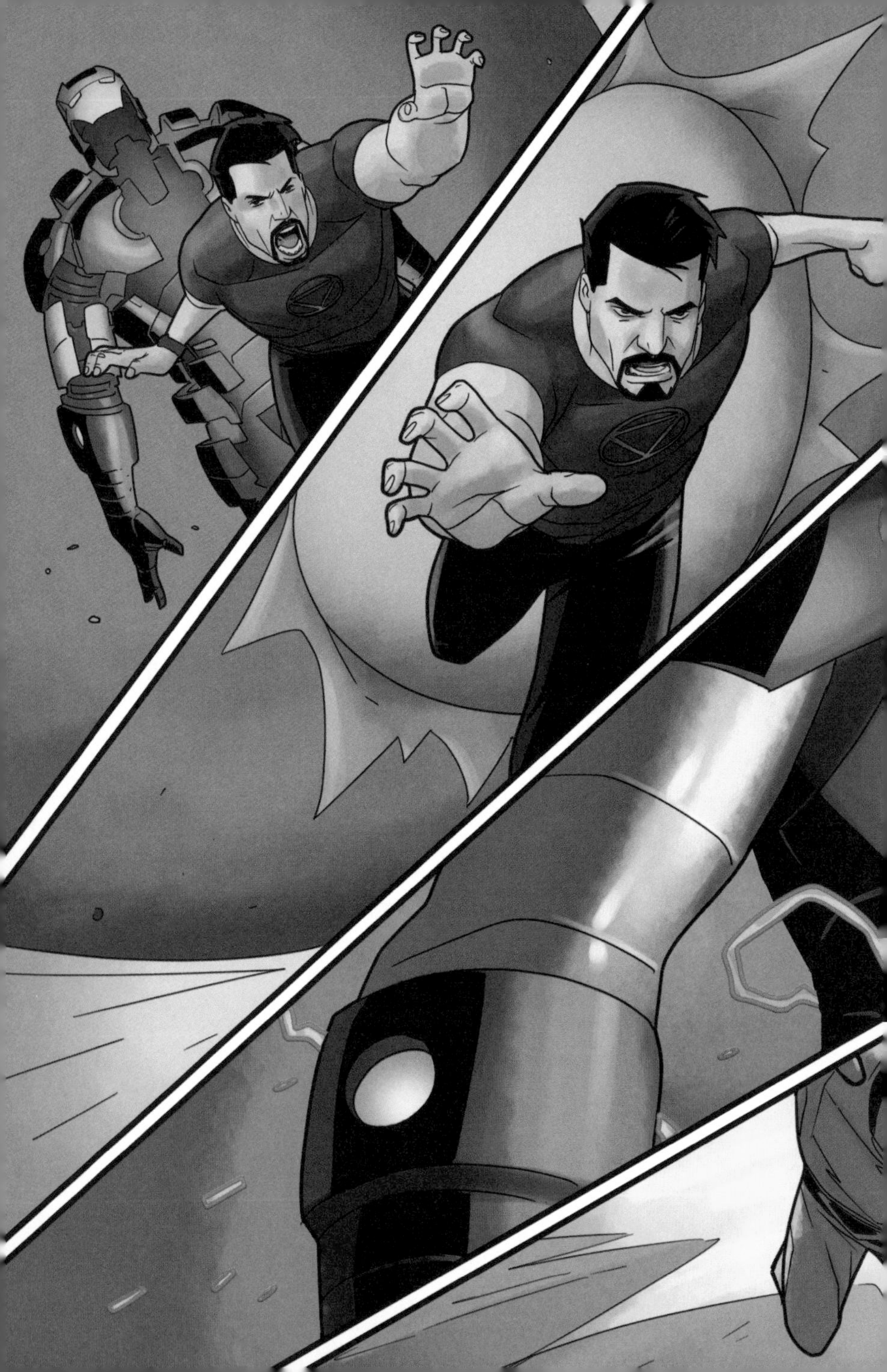

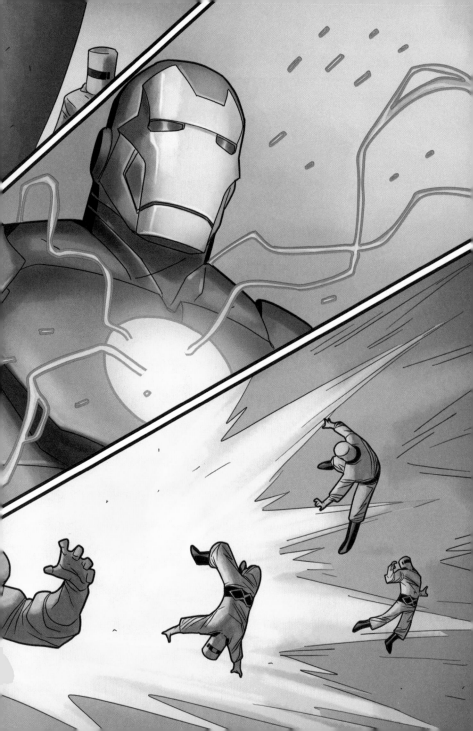

A dazed Tony Stark was the only one who had seen the explosion coming, and even he was surprised. *Who knew it would work that well?* thought Tony. He had deduced that the hard-light bubble was keyed to his armor and his

armor only—so ejecting himself from the armor effectively freed him. And by rerouting all the power to his unibeam, Tony overloaded the armor, causing it to self-destruct. He had bought himself precious time but at a price.

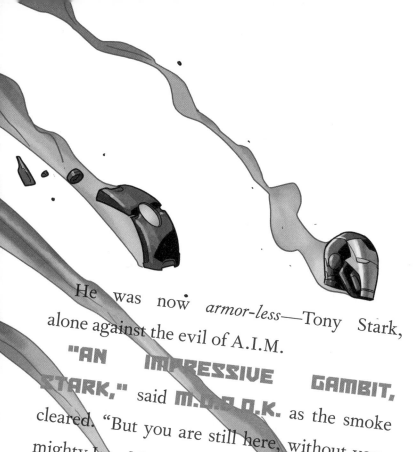

He was now *armor-less*—Tony Stark, alone against the evil of A.I.M.

"AN IMPRESSIVE GAMBIT, STARK," said **M.O.D.O.K.** as the smoke cleared. "But you are still here, without your mighty Iron Man armor. Surely a man as smart as you knows when to admit defeat."

Tony crouched behind a rack in the corner of the room. *I may not have my armor, but I'm still Tony Stark,* he thought. *And the day I let a bunch of beekeepers, goofy aliens, and a giant head stop me will be the day I can't memorize pi to seventy thousand places.*

"SHOW YOURSELF, STARK!" called **M.O.D.O.K.** "It is hopeless! Surrender now and I promise you a slow, agonizing death."

"That all sounds great, M.O.D.O.K.!" Tony yelled. **"It's a tempting offer, but I'll pass!"**

Tony was in trouble and he knew it. If only he had listened to Cap.

And that's when he heard it—**a distant rumbling**. The rumbling got **louder** and

louder. Everything in the room began to shake. Tiles fell from the ceiling and pillars toppled. Behind M.O.D.O.K., the wall burst in a great explosion!

Standing in the ruin was a large brutish figure, dripping wet, fists clenched. Through gritted teeth, the green-skinned monster snarled, **"Puny wall."**

OW

CHAPTER 9

"*H*ulk!" yelled Tony. The giant looked at Tony and grimaced. Or maybe it was a smile. It was kind of hard to tell. **"Smash!"**

The **Hulk** ran head-on into the sea of **A.I.M.** agents, their weapons blazing. The Hulk shrugged and tossed agents left and right. One landed next to Tony.

"Enough!" commanded **M.O.D.O.K.**, and his voice seemed to fill every part of the room. A beam of light issued from his headband, blasting the Hulk in the face. The Hulk roared in anger, then collapsed to the ground, holding his head.

A Phantom turned toward the **Cosmic Bridge Generator**. It moved its fingers over the watch on its wrist and the generator came to life. It glowed red, and creepy humanoid shapes began to emerge from within.

More Phantoms.

"Good to see you guys!" said Tony as the Phantoms advanced toward him.

"Who are you talking to, human?" asked a Phantom as it morphed its arm into a tentacle and wrapped it around Tony.

Tony gasped, **"Over . . . there."**

The Phantom sneered, "What are y—" then caught Captain America's shield in the face and lost its grip on Tony.

"We didn't follow you all the way from Antarctica to let one of those things get you," said Cap as **Falcon** and **Black Widow** took the fight to **A.I.M.** Tony smiled at his teammates. *I'm one lucky shellhead,* he thought, *lucky to have friends who've always got my back.*

"Never mind that," replied Tony. "*These* aliens plan on using *this* generator to invade our world!"

"So let's blow it to pieces!" said Black Widow, knocking an A.I.M. agent to the ground.

"Tried it. It's made out of some kind of material that isn't blow-up-able."

"Is that even a word?" asked Falcon, punching an **A.I.M.** agent through the helmet.

Cap smiled at Tony.

"So if force alone won't do it, what will?"

"Teamwork," offered Tony. "We can start by helping the Hulk. Can you take out M.O.D.O.K.'s psi-beam?"

After assessing the situation, **Captain America** had only to look at **Falcon**.

With the speed of his namesake, Falcon swooped in from above, raking one of his hard-light wings against **M.O.D.O.K.**'s face. His attack against the Hulk cut short, M.O.D.O.K. found himself face to face with Falcon's fury!

The **A.I.M.** agents scrambled to aid their fallen leader, but they had their own problem in the form of **Black Widow**! Like a one-woman wrecking crew, she tore through the agents. Using all the martial arts prowess at her command, Widow attacked relentlessly, never slowing.

"Cap! I know how we can stop these guys . . ." but I'm gonna need your help," said Tony. The two raced toward their green-skinned teammate.

"That's what friends are for," said Cap.

━●━

Cap and Tony were cut off from the Hulk. A line of Phantoms formed between them, shape-shifting into gruesome monsters. They looked like dinosaurs gone horribly wrong. Sharp talons, fangs, spiked tails, and long sinewy limbs. The creatures let loose an unearthly sound and continued to close in on the heroes.

"Puny monsters," growled the Hulk, smashing his enormous fists into the ground and sending the creatures flying.

"Can you keep these things busy, Hulk?" asked Tony. The Hulk grunted, grabbing one of the Phantoms by its tail. He whirled it around his head, then let go.

"So that's a yes," said Tony. "Come with me, Cap!"

Captain America ran alongside Tony and they slid to a stop at the base of the generator.

Tony shook his head. "The generator can transport *things* from the Phantoms' home world to Earth and vice versa. **But what happens if we program the generator to transport *itself*?**"

"I give up," Cap said. "What happens?"

"I don't know," replied Tony. **"But I'll bet you a brand-new space bike the Phantoms will hate it."**

———◉———

A no-holds-barred brawl raged in **A.I.M.** headquarters. **M.O.D.O.K.** tried in vain to hit Falcon with his psi-beam as the winged hero circled above. Black Widow continued her assault against the A.I.M. agents. There were only a few left standing at that point. Meanwhile, the Hulk smashed monster after monster.

I'll need you to throw your shield into the generator on my mark!" shouted Tony. Cap just looked at him. "Don't worry, you'll get it back!"

The star-spangled Avenger moved like a **RED-WHITE-AND-BLUE** blur, knocking back the alien invaders. "Whatever you're going to do, do it fast!"

Tony's fingers raced along the generator's controls. *Just a few seconds,* thought Tony. *Just a few seconds . . .*

"NOW!" cried Tony, and Cap hurled his shield into the Cosmic Bridge Generator just as the giant machine hummed to life. The shield hit the crackling red energy, and the entire room glowed red.

—◦—

As the red veil lifted from the room, Tony Stark looked around. He saw Cap's shield resting on the floor. The generator was gone— and along with it, every last trace of the

Phantoms . . . and M.O.D.O.K., too. All that remained were the Avengers and the defeated agents of A.I.M.

"Well, what do you know," Tony said. "It worked!"

"What did you do?" asked Cap, picking up his shield.

"I used your Vibranium shield to reflect the generator's energies on itself," Tony explained. "The generator has transported itself, along with the Phantoms and M.O.D.O.K. . . . somewhere in space and time."

CHAPTER

10

A few hours later, Tony Stark and Steve Rogers found themselves in an elevator aboard the **S.H.I.E.L.D.** Helicarrier. As the doors to the Helicarrier bridge opened, Tony and Steve walked inside. As usual, the place was buzzing with activity. Standing in the middle of it all was **Nick Fury**, the director of **S.H.I.E.L.D.**

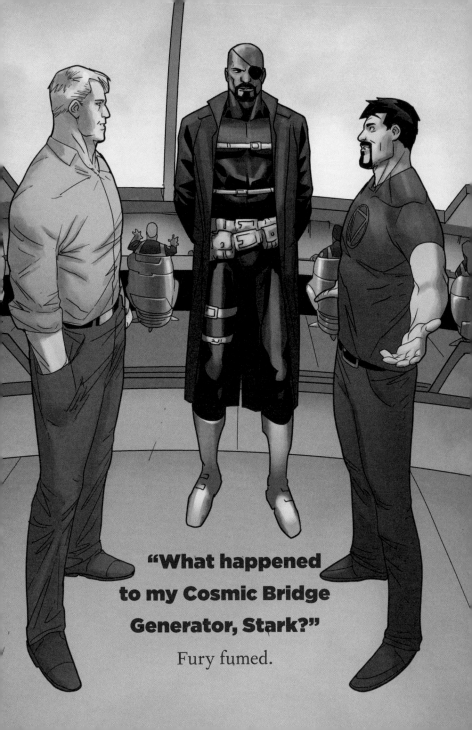

"What happened to my Cosmic Bridge Generator, Stark?" Fury fumed.

"Hi, Nick. How was your day?" Tony replied. Fury just stared at him.

"Technically, it's *my* generator. I made it," said Tony. "Since nobody could play with it nicely, I did the responsible thing. I took my ball and went home—so to speak."

"You're just lucky you stopped another alien invasion," Fury responded, turning his attention back to the bridge. "Otherwise, I might be mad. Plus, you

saved all of those brainwashed scientists."

"At first those scientists were creepy, but they were actually an impressive bunch. Oh, and I hate to correct you again, but *I* didn't stop another alien invasion and save Earth. *We* did. You know, teamwork?" Tony said.

Tony took in the view from the **S.H.I.E.L.D.** Helicarrier's observation deck. He could see all of New York City. Among the skyscrapers, he saw **STARK TOWER**. Home.

Amazing, thought Tony. *All of this would have been ruled by a bunch of pointy-headed aliens because I had to do everything on my own. Without the Avengers, my invention could have wiped out our planet.*

"Can I join you?" Steve Rogers walked onto the observation deck. "We got lucky today. We saved everyone at **OUTPOST 13**, and **S.H.I.E.L.D.** has taken the A.I.M. agents into custody. All that *and* we sent **M.O.D.O.K.** and an army of evil aliens packing."

"**M.O.D.O.K.** will be back. He always comes back," said Tony softly. "We would have been luckier if I had listened to you and Coulson."

Steve grinned warmly. "It never hurts to have a plan, and friends to make it happen."

"Y'know, Rogers, if this Super Hero thing doesn't work out, you could make a lot of money writing greeting cards," Tony said with a laugh.

It sounded lame, but Steve was right. Some problems couldn't be solved by Iron Man alone. Tony was part of a team—the mighty Avengers. He had their backs, and they had his.

There just might be something to this teamwork thing, he thought.

Motioning with his thumb toward the door, Steve said, **"Come on. You owe me shawarma *and* a new space bike."**